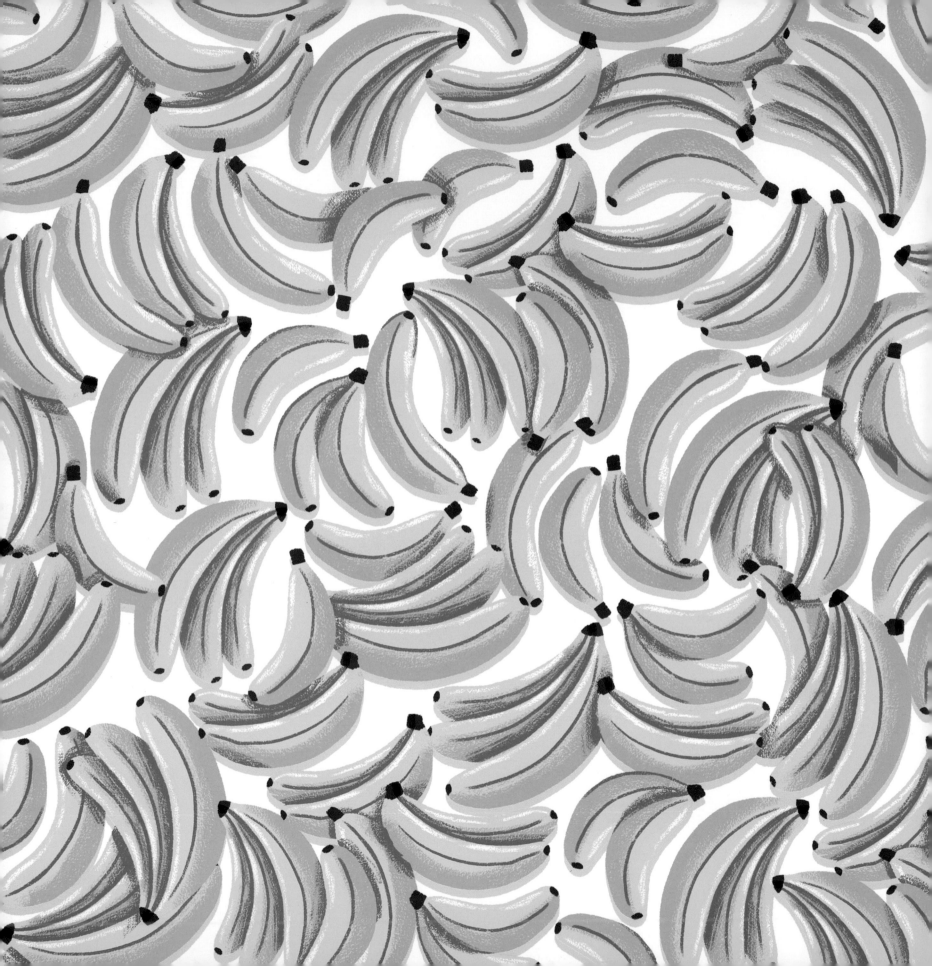

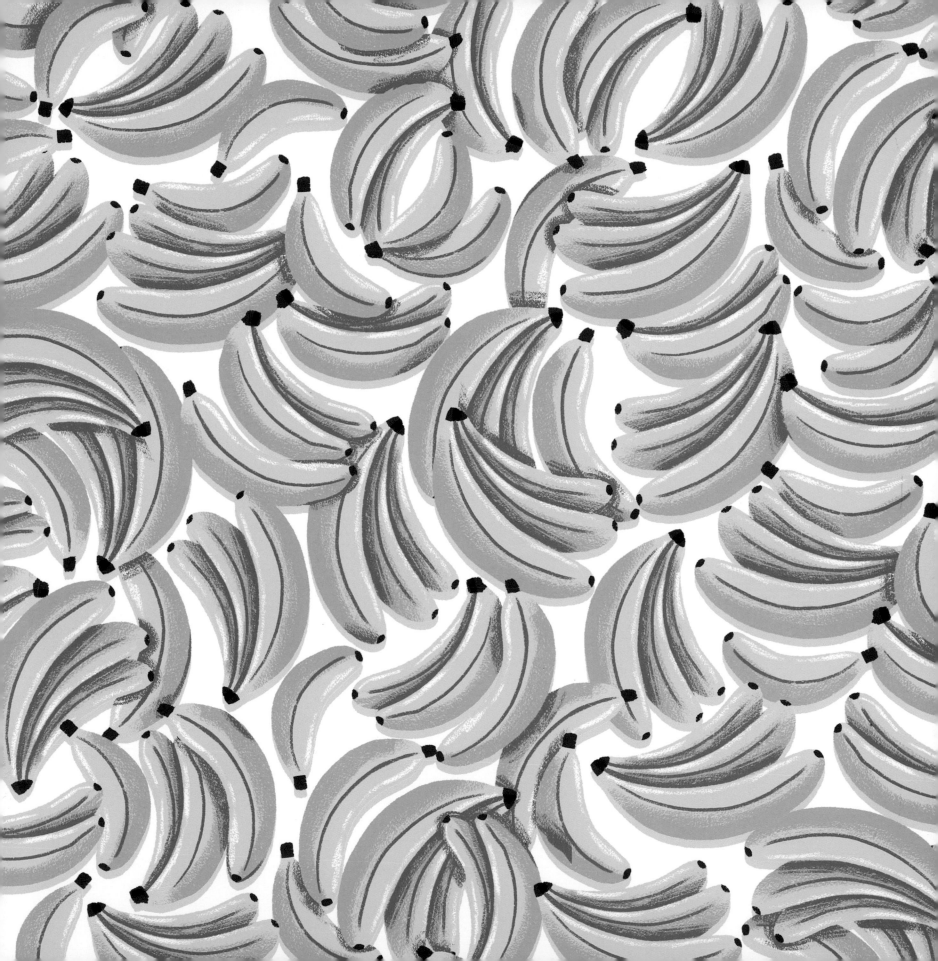

IMAGINE THAT™

Licensed exclusively to Imagine That Publishing Ltd
Tide Mill Way, Woodbridge, Suffolk, IP12 1AP, UK
www.imaginethat.com
Copyright © 2019 Imagine That Group Ltd
All rights reserved
4 6 8 9 7 5 3
Manufactured in China

Written by Benjamin Richards
Illustrated by Louise Forshaw

ISBN 978-1-78958-451-6

A catalogue record for this book is available from the British Library

For Dad, the cheekiest monkey I know

Written by Benjamin Richards
Illustrated by Louise Forshaw

Somewhere deep in the jungle, high up in the trees, lived two monkeys.

Milo

Mia

One morning, when Milo woke up, he had a horrible feeling. A feeling that he had forgotten something very, VERY important.

So he started
to think ...

He had remembered to do some exercise a few days ago ...

... and he had groomed Mia's fur the day after that ...

... and just yesterday, he'd tidied up all the banana skins at the bottom of their tree.

Suddenly Milo remembered ... he had forgotten it was Mia's birthday! And he hadn't got her a present!

Milo crept away to find a present for Mia before she woke up. He knew just what to get her — a banana.

Mia LOVED bananas. When she wasn't eating bananas, she was thinking about them. And when she wasn't thinking about bananas, she was eating them!

Milo quickly swung from tree to tree, and before long he found what looked like a brilliant birthday banana.

But it was MASSIVE.

'This banana is way too big,' said Milo.
'I'll never be able to carry it home!'

Milo swung to another tree and soon found another banana.

But this time it was way too small. In fact, it was teeny-tiny. 'Mia won't want this banana,' said Milo. 'She could eat it all in one bite!'

Then Milo spotted a HUGE bunch of
bananas that had fallen from a tree.
'What's better than one banana?
A whole bunch of them!' Milo shouted happily.

But, as he grabbed one of the bananas,
it squished and squelched in his hand.

'Mia can't eat these bananas,' groaned Milo.
'They are all mouldy.'

Milo found all sorts of bananas around the jungle.

Oi!

But no matter where he looked ...

... he couldn't find the perfect birthday banana for Mia.

Milo knew Mia would be awake soon.
He couldn't let her wake up on her
birthday without a present.

Milo grabbed the next banana he saw, and swung his way home as fast as he could.

Mia was just starting to wake up as Milo arrived home.

'Happy birthday, Mia!' called Milo.
'Thank you, Milo!' replied Mia.

But Mia noticed that something was wrong. 'Are you okay, Milo?'

'No,' said Milo. 'I couldn't find the perfect banana for your birthday present. I'm sorry, Mia.'

'Don't be silly,' said Mia.
'The most important thing is that you're here,
with me, on my birthday.'

'Why don't we share this banana?' said Mia.
'It'll be the perfect birthday breakfast.'

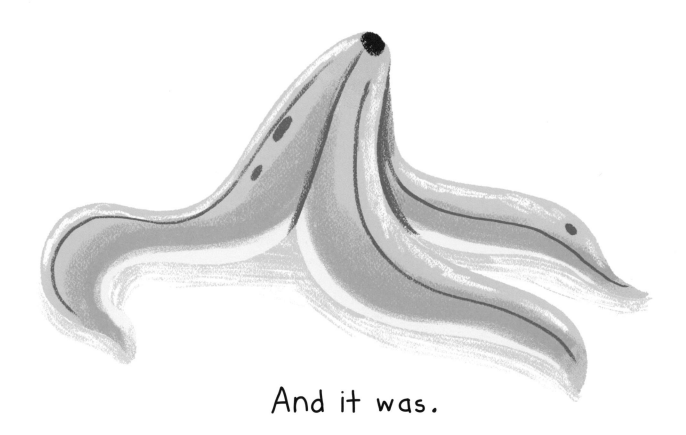

And it was.

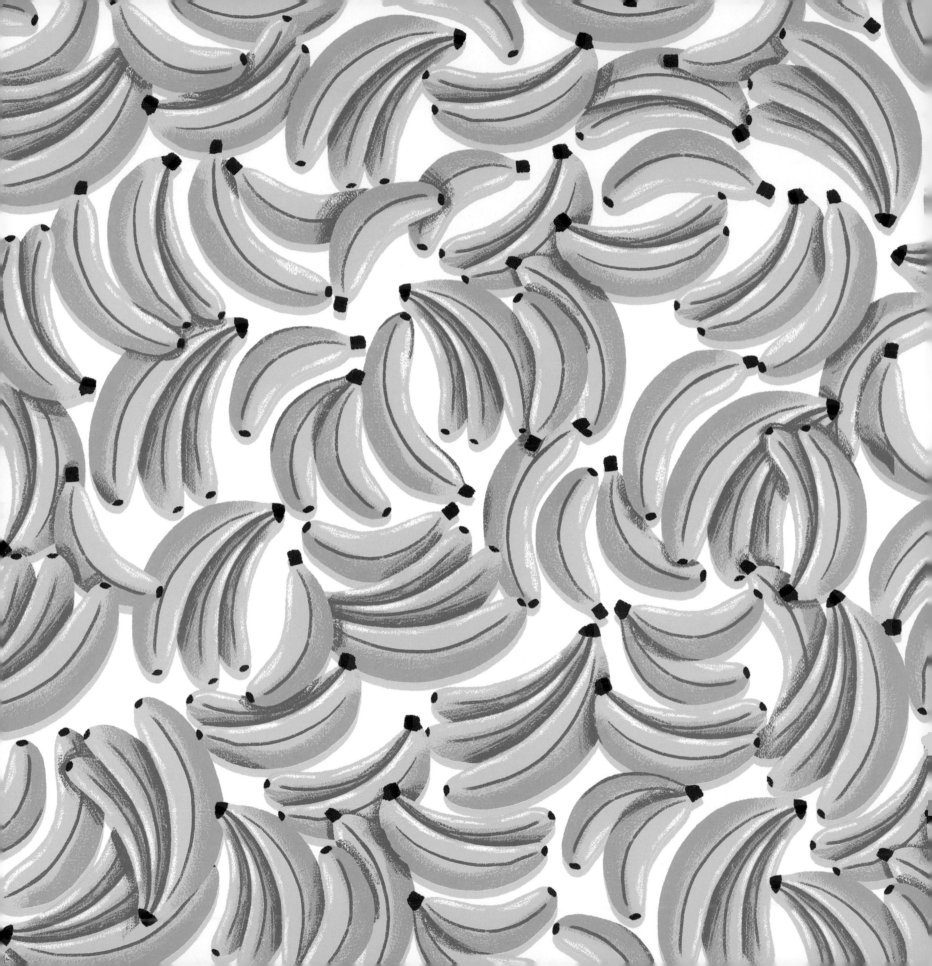

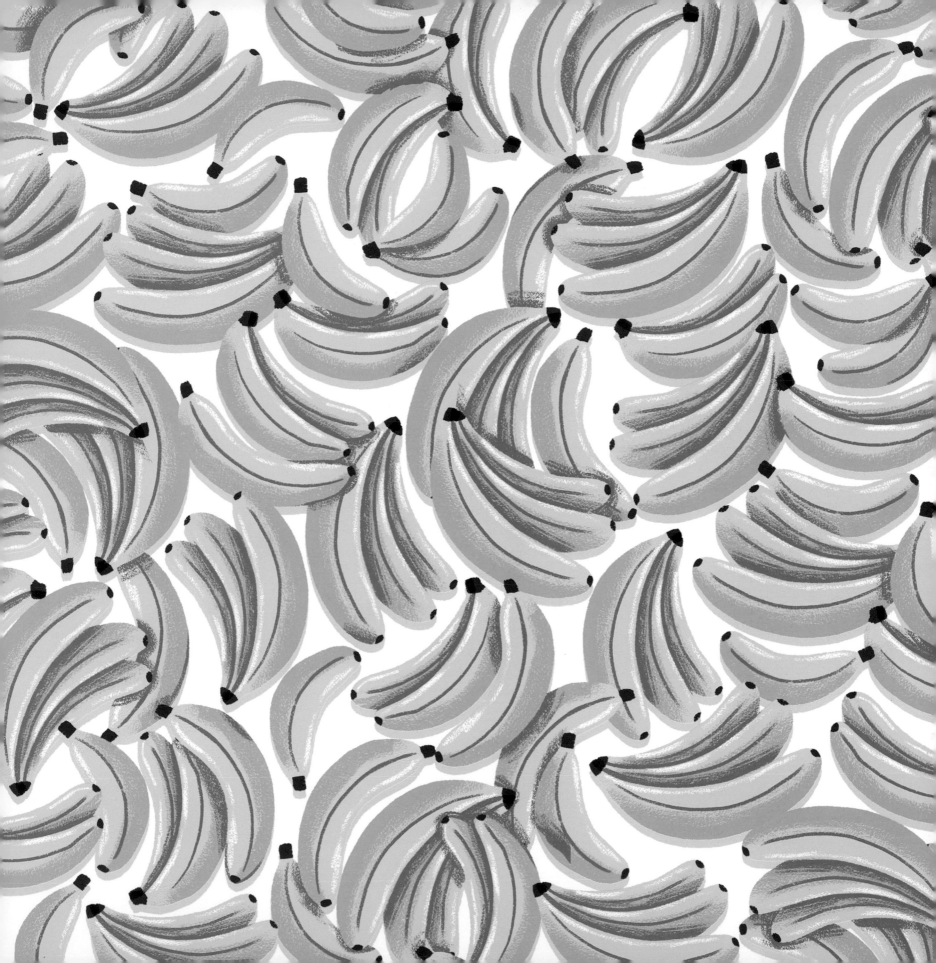